THE REAL GHOSTBUSTERS™

You Can't Take It With You

Maureen Spurgeon

Night had fallen on New York City. The streets were deserted, quiet and, for once, spook-free. The people of the great metropolis slept peacefully in their beds, secure in the knowledge that *should* any ectoplasmic eruption occur, The Real Ghostbusters would be there to save the world.

In Ghostbusters HQ, three of our heroes were also in bed *trying* to sleep peacefully. Winston Zeddmore had his head under the pillow counting ghosts jumping over the containment unit, Ray Stantz had his eyes shut tight and was trying to conjure up pictures of super-size-with-extra-topping pizzas. Peter Venkman was groaning. Loudly. And Egon Spengler? He was sitting up, reading the newspaper – aloud – and keeping everyone else awake.

"It's incredible really," he was saying. "The sheer nerve of it. Imagine *buying* the Empire State Building."

"Yeah – incredible," groaned Peter. "Go to sleep Egon – please!"

"It says here," Egon continued, "that this Tummel character is the richest man in America. Apparently his wealth runs to billions of dollars."

"Wrap up, Egon, " came the muffled voice of Winston from under his pillow. "Please."

Suddenly, one of their PKE meters began bleeping, and they looked round at each other, puzzled. A Psycho Kinetic Energy reading signalled the presence of some strange manifestation – but the question was – what? All had looked calm when they went to bed.

"Most peculiar . . ." murmured Egon. He went to pick the PKE meter up, but the bleeping had already stopped. "Most peculiar!"

Complete and utter silence. Then suddenly, all the alarms began echoing right the way through the entire building!

"The containment!" yelled Ray, already sliding down the fireman's pole to the basement, where all the ghost traps were unloaded. "Sounds like a major break!"

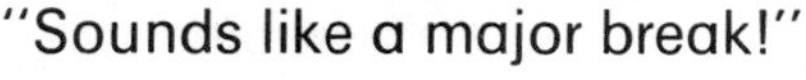

And, yet when Egon and Ray arrived at the containment unit everything seemed normal. Except that is for the lights on their PKE meters winking on and off, and a powerful buzzing noise that threatened to deafen them at any minute.

Then – silence again, just like before. None of them could understand it.

Meanwhile, in the roof-top laboratory of the Empire State Building, a bent, old man in a wheelchair was giving the final orders to his very own scientist. And, boy, could he afford to! For this was R. A. Tummel himself, the richest billionaire of them all!

"Ready to attempt transit, Sir!" the scientist announced, his hand poised over a Big Switch.

"Then, proceed!" wheezed Tummel. His beady eyes gleamed as dials glowed and sparks shot out from the top of a huge, silver pyramid in the middle of the room.

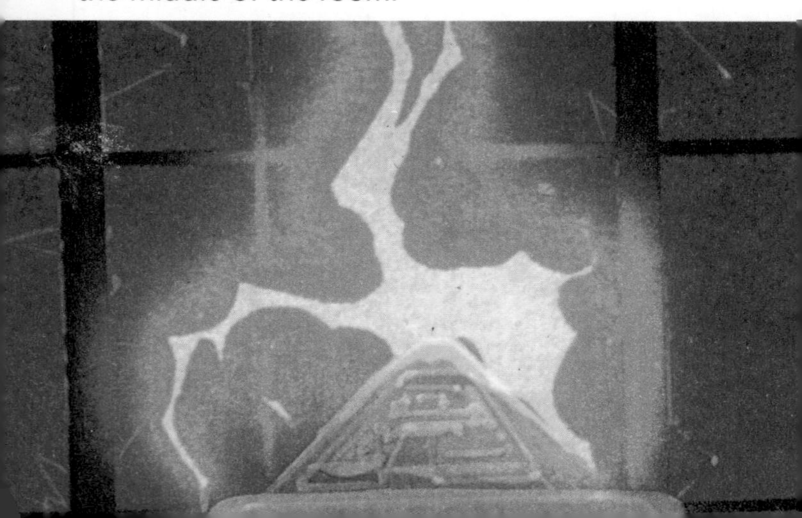

The four Ghostbusters screeched to a halt outside the building in the converted ambulance they called ECTO-1. They had followed the intermittent bleepings from their PKE meters until they had arrived at the Tummel skyscraper. It seemed as though the whole town was lit by the tornado of ectoplasm shooting up into the night sky, the top of the skyscraper swathed in a strange, glowing mist.

R. A. Tummel was certainly making sure the scientist earned his keep . . .

Already, a robot-controlled fork-lift had taken a whole conveyor belt load of gold bullion, and set it beneath the pyramid. Now, high above, the scientist was at the control panel . . .

"Hurry up!" Tummel snapped impatiently. "Get on with it!"

Wave upon wave of a glowing red light surged through the laboratory, spreading all around in one mighty roar. The gold bullion began shimmering, becoming transparent . . . then surging into a golden light it shot up towards a cluster of fast-whirling clouds . . .

"We did it!" cried the scientist. "We have transmitted gold – physical matter – into the ghost world!"

"Good!" Tummel cackled in delight. "Now I'll be able to take my whole fortune with me! Send over the next load!"

"But-but, Sir . . ." stammered the scientist. "We have to check to see what effect there has been on the environment . . ."

"Environment?" screeched Tummel. "Who

cares about the environment?"

"But-but, Mr Tummel . . ." Even as the man spoke, Tummel was jabbing a button on his wheel-chair. "We-we agreed that . . ."

He said no more. Two of Tummel's bodyguards had answered his call. They pounced on the scientist and dragged him away.

"Scientists!" Tummel spat out in disgust, a wrinkled hand reaching towards a portable control-box. "Who needs them?"

The roaring sound was even louder with the second lot of bullion. A steaming cloud of gold blasted up through the top of the pyramid with a noise like a thunderclap – a thunderclap merging into a chorus of unearthly wails which threatened to tear the night air apart.

The Ghostbusters had seen many, many strange things. But, never before had they seen a stream of ghostly ectoplasm shooting into the top of a skyscraper from a whirlpool of swirling cloud.

"Wh-what's that howling sound?" Peter asked at last, hardly daring to hear the answer.

"It's the wail of ghosts," Egon told him. "Hundreds and hundreds of ghosts! Whoever opened the door to the spirit world forgot that it swings both ways!"

"Which means the ghosts are coming back out!" groaned Peter. "I don't believe it!"

Tummel could hardly believe it, either. Everywhere he looked, there were ghosts coming towards him from the direction of the

pyramid, whirling and swirling around, screaming and grunting and wailing.

Lucky for Tummel, his scientist had left him well prepared. He pressed a switch on his wheelchair and a whole set of curved rods shot out from the arms, joining up above his shrivelled head like a giant, glowing phone-booth.

Another switch – and up came a Proton Gun from the back of the wheelchair, swivelling around on a tall rod, firing in all directions.

"Go on!" shrieked Tummel, enjoying the sight of so many spooks, all screaming and yelling at once, and flooding out through the door. "Beat it, you creeps!"

Down on the street, The Ghostbusters ran for their lives as a whole swarm of gruesome ghosts, ghoulies and spooks teemed onto the pavement. Egon dived into a nearby hedge for safety, Ray found himself flattened against a lamp-post.

Winston peered from behind a trash-can where he had lunged for safety.

"I think," he said, "we'd better get up there . . ."

That was easier said than done. The moment they set foot inside the building, Egon's PKE meter began buzzing like crazy – signalling the approach of four gruesome ghosts heading straight towards them!

Proton beams from four Proton Guns streaked out instantly, hitting two of the ghosts. As for the other two, they flew clean over The Ghostbusters' heads and into the darkness, mists trailing behind.

Egon took a deep breath, and looked around. "These ghosts are coming through from the spirit world by artificial means," he said. "They could break up, each fragment becoming a complete ghost . . ."

"Then, the cycle could repeat?" Peter queried slowly. "The world could become full of ghosts?"

"Yes." Egon was deadly serious. "In about fifteen hours. I think we'd better take the stairs . . ."

"Are you crazy?" demanded Peter. "It's 150 floors, and . . . Egon, why are you looking like that? Can't you do anything but point? What the . . .?"

He glanced over his shoulder and suddenly understood. A huge, giant mouth was where the

lift doors had been.

"Aaaaagh!" yelled Peter, narrowly escaping a long, red tongue. All the lift doors yawned wide open to reveal huge, watering mouths, hungrily champing monster teeth, and enormous, slobbering lips.

"Come on!" Ray Stantz was bellowing. 'Get into ECTO-2!"

The ghostly cloud still whooshed up from inside the building, tossing ECTO-2, The Ghostbusters' helicopter, around like a rag doll, high above the towering Tummel skyscraper.

"We-we're fighting the magnetic pull of the ghost world!" Ray panted, struggling to keep control, and yelling above the bolts of electricity which were crackling all around, like huge forks of lightning.

Next minute – total silence. The deadly quiet made The Ghostbusters glance fearfully at each other.

"The magneto's been hit!" yelled Ray. "We're losing height!"

"Rip the wires from the instrument panel, Ray!" shouted Egon. "I'll try connecting them into my Proton Pack!"

Ray hurriedly made a jump-lead to connect up to the ignition. He turned the key, and, in the nick of time, the helicopter gave a lurch and the rotor blades began whirling again.

In a matter of moments, The Ghostbusters had landed on the rooftop. They bundled out of ECTO-2, yelling their heads off, their Proton Guns firing at the army of spooks who had been

waiting for the attack.

"Okay, you guys!" roared Peter to the others, once the coast was clear. "Inside!"

The Tummel skyscraper really was some cool place. Paintings . . . statues . . . tons of stuff made of solid gold . . . But The Ghostbusters had no time for an inspection tour. They headed straight for Tummel's sky-high laboratory.

"So!" shrieked Tummel, as the alarms sounded. "I have uninvited guests!"

"Mr Tummel!" called Egon. "Could we have a word with you?"

"No!" screeched Tummel, glaring down at them from the observation balcony. "Have a word with these, instead!"

"Lasers!" gasped Winston, looking up at the ceiling, where the powerful beams were swivelling around, searching for their targets.

"High power lasers! Take cover!"
They were only just in time. Winston had hardly pushed Ray away when a beam of ruby light zapped down, right where he had been standing, leaving a molten, smoking hole.
"Ha!" snarled Tummel, positively enjoying all the bangs, the explosions, the smoke and the flashes. "That should keep them busy! Time for the money to go across, I think!"
"Wow . . ." Egon couldn't help being impressed as he watched huge bundles of bank-notes glowing, becoming transparent, then being sucked up into the pyramid in a stream of gold vapour. "That's fantastic!"
"Never mind how fantastic it is!" snapped Peter. "How do we get him to stop?"
"If we could only get him to overload his equipment . . ." Egon said thoughtfully, specs gleaming. "That would block the whole works!"
Peter thought quickly, then tied a handkerchief to the barrel of his Proton Gun. "You've blown it, Tummel!" he shouted, waving the makeshift white flag. "You can send over your loot, but what about this building? Where are you going to live? They don't have hotels over there you know. Leaving it to charity?"
"Charity?" roared Tummel. "Never! I'm taking it with me!"
The whole laboratory began throbbing with a huge roar: the deadly laser beams went berserk. Clearly, Tummel meant every word he said.
"He's overloading the equipment, Egon!" said Peter. "What now?"

But even an ace Ghostbuster like Egon Spengler could not have predicted what happened next. A stray laser shot hit the switch panel on Tummel's wheelchair, sending it straight down the ramp which led towards the pyramid!

"No! Wait!" shrieked Tummel, frightened out of his life. But, it was hopeless. With one last, loud "No-o-o-o-o . . ." the wheelchair rolled under the pyramid.

As one man, The Ghostbusters ran forward, even though, deep down, they each knew they could do nothing to help . . .

"The system's running wild!" bawled Egon.

"Shoot the controls!" bellowed Peter, taking aim along with Winston.

"It's too late!" shouted Ray. "The system's on automatic!"

Impulsively, Egon made a grab at the ghost trap and began racing forward, dodging the hail of laser fire. Holding his breath, he opened the doors to the ghost trap, then pushed hard, skidding it across the laboratory floor and under the pyramid.

Almost immediately, there was an ear-splitting warbling noise and waves of light started to flash madly. Two laser shots almost hit Egon before Winston managed to snatch at his belt and pull him to safety. He was just in time. A split second later a huge chunk of Tummel's laboratory came crashing down, and landed right where he had been standing.

"The ghost trap should jam the transmission works!" panted Egon, as The Ghostbusters began sprinting towards the living quarters for safety. "I-I only hope it's enough to pull back the ghosts which Tummel released, and close the hole!"

Three deathly-white faces emerged from the living room. Only this time they weren't ghosts, they were Tummel's butler, cook and gardener, their frightened staring eyes lit by the streaks of lightning which flashed through the windows.

"Oh, thank goodness!" cried the butler. "Mr. Tummel was going to send us into the ghost world, along with all his riches!"

"Well, that's all over, now!" Egon told them, staring up at the sky, and the hordes of ghosts rising towards the distant clouds. "All the spirits are going back through the gate . . ."

"So is this building in about thirty seconds!" interrupted Peter, dragging Egon, the butler, cook and gardener towards the helicopter. For a moment, they were all thrown off balance, and

Peter had to reach out to steady himself.

His hand passed straight through solid brickwork.

"This is it, Peter," Egon nodded, "The building's molecular structure is beginning to disintegrate!"

"Hurry up!" yelled Ray from the cockpit of ECTO-2. "Quick, before she goes!"

By now, the skyscraper was throbbing beneath the swirling cloud, tongues of burning vapour missing the helicopter by inches.

In near desperation, Winston ripped off his Proton Pack and flung it down towards the glowing building. The massive blast which followed lasted just long enough for ECTO-2 to break free from the deadly magnetic pull . . .

"Look!" Egon shouted. "It's Tummel!"

And, so it was, rising into the air in a cackle of mad laughter, along with all the other ghosts. Seconds later his skyscraper was sucked up, vanishing in a thunderous explosion which almost split the whole sky into two.

How Ray Stantz landed the helicopter safely, nobody ever knew.

"Now, who'd believe that?" he said dazedly. "The Tummel skyscraper, gone, and . . . Ow!" He rubbed his head indignantly. "What hit me?"

"Well, what d'you know?" grinned Peter Venkman, as bundles of notes and gold bars began showering down. "Tummel may have been a real meanie, but it seems this job's going to pay better than we ever thought!"

THE MAN WHO NEVER REACHED HOME

It was a strange, half-forgotten tale. How, over 100 years ago, a man named Simon Quegg strode from a roadside inn, threatening to have it closed. The innkeeper pleaded with him to change his mind. But Quegg would not listen. Instead he mounted his horse buggy, determined to leave the place at once and travel home. The innkeeper warned him of the danger of travelling on such a terrible night, when thunder rolled and lightning flashed across the sky, but it was no use.

"The devil himself can't stop me!" Quegg had ranted. "Or, may I never see home again!" And with that he hurtled off into the night.

At once a flash of lightning cracked down from the sky, hitting the ground where Quegg's carriage had been. In its place was a horse, dark as the night itself with glowing eyes, spurred on by a black, faceless rider. The horse reared up and then the rider spurred it on down the road – in pursuit of Quegg.

Simon Quegg was never seen again after that dreadful, stormy night. And it was a similar night that faced The Ghostbusters as they returned from one of their missions. Ray Stantz was at the wheel of ECTO-1, with his green ghosty-friend, Slimer, up there on his shoulder.

Peter, Egon and Winston knew that Ray was just a big kid at heart. They knew he always felt sorry for Slimer whenever he was scolded by Peter, or left out of things in general. So, it came as no surprise when they stopped at a coffee shop, and Ray ordered two dozen hamburgers to take-out, just for the little green ghoulie, left behind in the Ectomobile.

The owner of the coffee shop may have raised an eyebrow or two – but, anyway, he reckoned, he needed the business. Stormy nights were usually bad for trade . . .

"We'll be out in a little while, Slimer!" Ray grinned, watching as the whole tray of hamburgers was shovelled into the ghosty-green mouth. It was good to see Slimer munching so happily.

Then, he stopped. Surely, Ray thought, that couldn't possibly be the sound of hooves pounding towards him, wheels rattling along the road?

"Whoa!" came a voice, and a horse-drawn buggy suddenly loomed out of the darkness. Ray could see an unhappy, haunted-looking

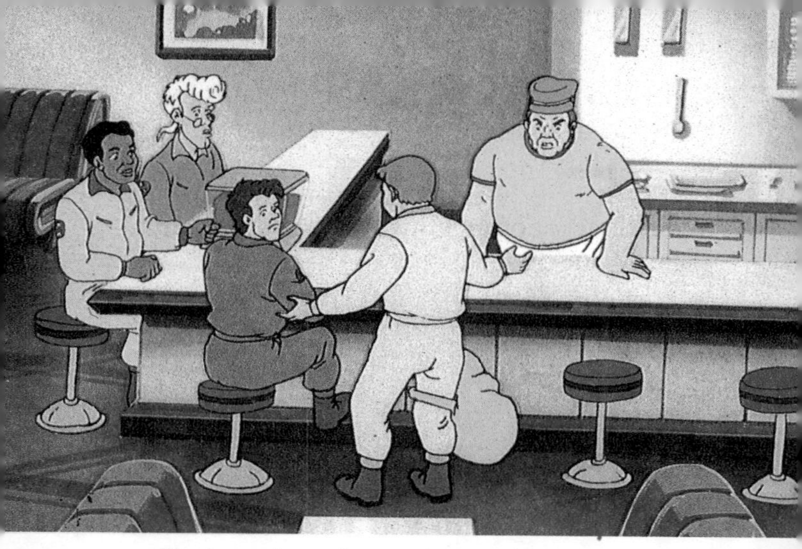

man pulling at the reins trying to keep the restless horse under control.

"Can you tell me, sir," – even the voice sounded haunted – "how many miles it is to my home at Providence?"

Ray was surprised. "Providence, Rhode Island? It's 80 miles east from here!"

"What? But, Providence was only 20 miles west, when I left the inn!"

"I'm telling you the truth!" Ray insisted. "You've got to turn around and go 80 miles back east!"

"No!" The man glanced back in terror. "I cannot tarry any longer! It gains on me every minute! Yet, I must reach home tonight!"

A crack of the reins, and both horse and buggy were gone.

Then – more hoof beats, echoing strangely through the night, hot blasts of steaming breath

. . . and a black-clad rider on horseback thundered past, making Slimer cling on to Ray for dear life.

"Slimer!" Ray yelled desperately, striding towards the coffee shop at the same time. "Slimer, let go!"

Dripping with rain, and with Slimer attached to his leg, Ray flung open the door. Peter, Egon and Winston were just finishing their coffee and hamburgers.

"Did you see them?" Ray demanded, a wild look in his eyes. "A man in old fashioned clothes, said he was trying to get to-to . . ."

"Providence?" finished the coffee shop owner. "That's just old Simon Quegg, our local ghost. Shows up on stormy nights, asking the way home, but never believes anyone when they tell him!"

"What about the other rider?" Ray persisted. "The one that followed Quegg?"

"You saw that?" Suddenly, the owner was a very frightened man.

"Well – yes."

"Only a handful of people have ever seen the Rider!" the man gabbled, bundling them all towards the door. "And disaster always follows! You've got to go!"

The door slammed, leaving The Ghostbusters staring blankly through the pouring rain, first at the "CLOSED" sign, then at each other.

"Come on!" yelled Winston, first to start running towards ECTO-1. "Let's get out of the rain!"

"Guys," said Stantz, once they were all safely inside, "we've just got to find this Simon Quegg. Tonight. I saw the terrified look in his eyes . . . And all he wants is to go home!"

"From a scientific viewpoint," said Egon, already peering behind his specs for some sign of life on his PKE meter, "it might be interesting . . ."

On and on, Ray Stantz drove the Ectomobile through the raging storm. Egon was about to suggest calling the whole thing off and going home, when the needle suddenly jumped to a maximum Psycho Kinetic Energy reading.

"Stop!" he yelled, waking up Peter and Slimer. "Stop here!"

The Ghostbusters barely had time to put on their Proton Packs, before the sound of galloping hooves, creaking wheels and the

jingling of a horse's harness mingled with the sound of the pouring rain. Egon Spengler was always right.

"Gentlemen, please let me pass!" cried Quegg, reining his horse to a stop. "I must reach home before the night is out!"

"You asked me directions a little while ago," said Ray. "Remember?"

"Yes . . ." Quegg nodded in confusion. "You-you told me that Providence was . . . that it was . . ." He gave a dreadful moan, covering his face with a trembling hand. "Oh, why can't I find my way home?"

"Maybe we can help you," Ray suggested, more gently. "Just get down from the buggy!"

"I don't think he can, Ray," Egon interrupted. "It and the horse happen to be more powerful than he is! The Psycho Kinetic Energy readings on the PKE meter are completely different!"

"Then," said Ray, adjusting his Proton Gun, "I'll have to trap the horse and buggy, without getting Quegg!"

"No!" screamed Quegg, already shaking the reins to get the horse moving. "I-I can hear it drawing closer, closer every minute . . ."

But Ray raised his gun and fired – right on target. Both the horse and the buggy began to glow brightly.

"Oh, no!" Egan looked up anxiously from his faithful PKE meter. "Ray, please stop! There's a danger of . . ."

His warning came only seconds too late. The proton beam bounced back and caught Ray, at the same moment as Quegg fell to the ground with a thump. And when the horse and buggy appeared again, they were carrying Ray Stantz away, into the darkness!

Then came the second, far more sinister sound of galloping hooves. A black horse and rider loomed out of nowhere, then soaring right above their heads, chased Ray on Quegg's ghost buggy.

Worse still, the night was lightening, soon it would be daybreak. Egon, Peter and Winston all knew there was no hope of finding Ray until dead of night, and only then if the weather was stormy again.

"I-I seem to remember . . ." They had almost forgotten! Quegg was still with them. "I have to return home . . ."

"Hey! You're not going anywhere!" cried Peter, poking a finger at him. "Ray risked his life to help you!"

"I did not ask for his help!" Quegg retorted. "Now, I must go in this direction . . . Or, is it that way? I don't . . . I don't know . . ."

"I think, Mr. Quegg," said Egon, "we have to help each other. You help us find Ray, and we'll help you get home!"

Not that Quegg *was* much help, as they soon discovered, back at the Ghostbusters' HQ.

"I've told you everything I know!" he kept saying irritably. Slimer lashed out at him every five minutes. There was no doubt he blamed Quegg for losing his friend.

The weather forecast didn't sound too hopeful, either. "Just a cloudy night!" Winston announced, following the umpteenth call to the weather station. "No rain or thunderstorms!"

"Have to make our own, then!" said Egon, coming in with a small tank, complete with a hose, nozzle and a control box on the side. "Just as soon as it's dark!"

"Yeah," said Winston, "but there's no guarantee Ray and the buggy will appear, just because we've created our own rain!" "Mr. Quegg is our guarantee," said Egon, his eyes firmly on the disgruntled ghost. "He's the one who belongs on that buggy, after all!"

At long last, it was time to return to the spot where Ray had disappeared. Everyone clambered into ECTO-1. Slimer was looking very pleased with himself – he had been given a special job to do.

"How can you make it rain?" Quegg couldn't help asking.

"See Egon's special device?" said Winston. "That's filled with silver iodide! Spray it on the right kind of clouds, and, if you're lucky – boom! It rains!"

There was a loud rumble, and out of the back of ECTO-1 roared ECTO-2, The Ghostbusters' helicopter, piloted by Egon Spengler. And, who should be the co-pilot? Why, none other than Slimer, complete with helmet and goggles, and squealing delightedly as the helicopter soared into the sky.

"You know what to do, Slimer?" asked Egon, after a few minutes.

Slimer nodded enthusiastically, turning the dial back and forth on Egon's tank-machine, and setting it on HIGH.

"Okay Slimer! Push the button!"

Swelling with importance, Slimer pointed the nozzle down over the side of the helicopter and pushed the button on the control box.

A strong blast of yellow powder shot out with such force that he was torn from his safety strap and launched into the air, Egon and ECTO-2 both tumbling towards the ground.

It was only by sheer guts and some good luck that Egon kept control of the helicopter – but Slimer was not so fortunate. All he could do was to hang on to Egon's rain-maker, a trail of yellow powder lacing through the clouds behind him, until the last puff of silver iodide was gone, and he fell out of the sky.

This time, his luck was in. He landed on something soft. Dr Peter Venkman to be precise, covering him with green slime – just as he'd done on Peter's first-ever ghostbusting job.

"Slimer!" he growled. He had never quite

forgiven the little green ghoul.
A huge fork of lightning followed by a loud crash of thunder made them all look up, rain was beginning to pour down by the bucket-load. Peter Venkman was soaked through in a matter of minutes!

"Someone talk me into finding another job!" he growled, with one last glare in Slimer's direction.

But the sound of galloping hooves and the creak of buggy wheels soon made him and the other two Ghostbusters hold their breath, hoping against hope that Ray Stantz would be on board the ghost ride.

And, so he was! Wide-eyed, worn out – but still in one piece!

"Boy!" he sighed. "Am I glad to see you guys?" He tried to dismount the buggy, but – as with Quegg – some strange force seemed to hold him back.

"No! Don't zap the buggy!" Ray cried out in alarm, seeing Winston's Proton Gun at the ready. "I tried that, and look where it got me!"

"Because you fired alone!" Egon shouted back. "If we fire our three proton beams all together, we should stand a better chance!"

So much for looking on the bright side . . . Three Proton Guns fired towards the horse and buggy – but nothing happened!

"The lightning must have overloaded our Proton Packs!" yelled Egon. "It's caused short circuits all round!"

"Maybe that's just what we should do!" Ray roared back at him, the black rider thundering nearer. "For so long, that rider has chased you, kept you from going home! So, break the cycle! Get back on the buggy with me, and we'll face him together!"

Nobody said anything. But, at that moment, everyone there realised what a brave little guy Ray Stantz actually was, including Quegg.

"Perhaps you are right, Mr Stantz," he nodded at last, climbing up and taking the reins from Ray's hands.

Meanwhile the black rider was galloping closer and closer . . .

"We must leave!" shrieked Quegg. Already they could hear the devilish horse and the black rider approaching. "We must not stay here!"

A sudden flash of lightning made the mysterious rider lift his head – and Simon Quegg could not have been more astounded.

"Th-that's my face!" he gasped, seeing the hideous lips, the evil smile. "I-I've been running away from – from myself!"

"Forgive me, Mr Stantz," he went on, pushing Ray down from the buggy. "But, I must do this alone!"

"Faster! Faster!" he yelled, cracking the reins like fury – until the two riders and two horses

met, passing right through each other.

There was a strong gust of wind, and a whirlpool of ectoplasmic material swirled up into the sky like a tornado, blowing the clouds and the rain away to reveal a clear bright moon.

And, through the beautiful, peaceful night, came the sound of a horse and buggy trotting along, Simon Quegg holding the reins.

"I had to come back and thank you, Mr Stantz," he smiled happily. "You gave me the courage to see that the rider was me – the cruel, selfish man I have always been. And now – now, Mr Stantz I can at last go home!"

Carnival
An imprint of the Children's Division
of the Collins Publishing Group
8 Grafton Street, London W1X 3LA

Published by Carnival 1989

ISBN 0 00 192340-4

Printed and bound in Great Britain by
BPCC Paulton Books Limited